PLAYS FOR PERFORMANCE

A series designed for
contemporary production and study
Edited by
Nicholas Rudall and Bernard Sahlins

LUIGI PIRANDELLO

Six Characters in Search of an Author

In a New Adaptation by
Robert Brustein and
The American Repertory Theatre Company

Ivan R. Dee
CHICAGO

Library of Congress Cataloging-in-Publication Data:
Brustein, Robert Sanford, 1927–
    Six characters in search of an author / Luigi Pirandello : in a new adaptation by Robert Brustein and The American Repertory Theatre Company.
        p. cm — (Plays for performance)
    ISBN 0-929587-62-6 (cloth : alk. paper). — ISBN 0-929587-58-8 (paper : alk. paper)
        1. Characters and characteristics in literature—Drama.
    2. Authorship—Drama. I. Pirandello, Luigi, 1867–1936. Sei personaggi in cerca d'autore. II. American Repertory Theatre. III. Title. IV. Series.
    PS3552.R845S5   1998
    812'.54—dc21   97-24711

INTRODUCTION

by Robert Brustein

This text was prepared for the American Repertory Theatre's production of *Six Characters* in Cambridge in the fall of 1996, the result of a continuing collaboration between the company actors and myself. The time and place are reflected in the adaptation, but the production has enjoyed a number of revivals, over a period of eight years, in various cities and with a variety of different actors, always adapted to changing conditions. This version, in other words, is meant to be liquid, spontaneous, improvisatory, adaptable—much like Pirandello's concept of the drama. Directors and actors are encouraged to treat it as loosely as I have treated the original text.

In Pirandello, the six characters intrude on actors rehearsing his own play *Mixing It Up*. In our version, they walk in on a rehearsal of *The King Stag*, a popular play in the ART repertory. In your own production, the play being rehearsed by the actors should, if possible, be a vehicle familiar to your audiences—say, *Our Town*, or *A Christmas Carol*. When the American Conservatory Theatre performed *Six Characters*, it announced a showing of *Hamlet*, and had the characters interrupt the opening scene.

Similarly, the ART actors in the play (aside from the six characters) used their own names, often their own characters and attitudes. Feel free to sub-

3

stitute the names of your own actors—and improvise with them asides and witticisms more appropriate to personal experience and local history.

A problem which this approach engenders is determining the nationality of the six characters. We treated them as essentially Italian, since Pirandello conceived them that way, with Italian concepts of honor and moral codes. The exception was Madame Pace, who (for company reasons—we were one woman short) was turned into a Latino pimp named Emilio Paz. An American city has lots of Latinos, but what are formally dressed Italians doing in a theatre filled with American actors? The answer is that they come from the author's imagination, but if your actors need more motivation (the audience doesn't), tell them the family are immigrants newly off the boat.

Six Characters depends a lot on magic, which is to say stage tricks. Although magicians are not supposed to disclose their secrets, here are some hints about the way we solved our problems. Avoid using a curtain. The audience walking in will see what appears to be an empty stage, decorated with flats and props stored up from other shows. Downstage left there is a table and chairs, where the stage manager is setting up for rehearsal—sharpening pencils, chalking the stage, instructing a stage hand, and so forth. At the back of the stage is a loading door (a painted drop if you don't have one) through which the characters enter.

The entrance of the actors poses no problems, and their banter and rehearsal should proceed under work lights until the director (Jeremy) complains that he needs better illumination. The scrim we used as the *The King Stag* backdrop began to tremble right before the entrance of the characters (use a wind machine), then went transparent.

When the loading door lifted slowly, revealing the six, they were brilliantly back lit, moving from side to side in unison. It is best to follow each of the six, but especially the Father, with a special light different in quality, intensity, and color from the lighting on the rest of the stage.

For the scene in the back room of Emilio Paz's grind house, we did the following. The Father and the Stepdaughter ask to set up the scene with furniture simulating the furniture of the room: a table (with the envelope on it), a couch, a clothes rack. The most important element is the mirror. We brought down a huge mirror from the flies, composed of a mylar material which was transparent when lights were used behind it. When Paz materialized behind the mirror, the furniture in the back room was exactly parallel to the crude props placed in front of the mirror. But the mylar was not only transparent—*it actually projected an image of the actor standing in front of the mirror back into the room.* Thus, when the Father and Stepdaughter sat down on the bench facing the front of the mirror, they seemed to be sitting facing us on the couch in the room; and when the Mother aimed her handbag at Paz behind the mirror, she actually seemed to have hit him in the face. Thus, scenes were played in front of and behind the mirror at once.

Pirandello uses a lot of narrative in this play. One way to make that narrative dramatic is to bring it into the present. When the Father and Stepdaughter tell of their encounter near her school when she was little, make that a scene that's actually happening, with the Father stroking her face while she tells (in a little girl's voice) about her reactions. Do the same thing when the Father narrates how the Stepdaughter entered his house (after the encounter in Paz's back room) and saucily demanded money.

The most difficult—and most effective—scene in the play is the last one. Having set up the light booms to simulate trees and the blue plastic to simulate a pond and a cardboard moon, the play proceeds. The Son—finally forced to speak—faces the audience and tells the story of how he watched the little girl go near the pond. The Mother crosses sorrowfully to join him. That cross brings the spectator's eye to focus on the little girl with the Stepdaughter standing behind her helplessly. Very slowly, the plastic on which the little girl is lying begins to descend (we used an elevator for the purpose) as the plastic fills with water, enough to drench her clothes. The Stepdaughter reaches down and, sobbing softly, brings the dripping body offstage.

As the Son continues his story, the scrim once again turns transparent to reveal a parallel reality behind the simulated stage props. The Boy is revealed standing by a real tree as a real moon casts its image on the pond at which he's looking. The Son (pointing his finger at his head) parallels the action of the Boy pointing a revolver at his head. The shot is fired, the Boy falls, the lights go out, and the actors rush behind the scrim as the rest of the family disappears off stage. Pandemonium ensues—shouts, screams, falling furniture. The only light is provided by an actor (Chuck) who brandishes a desk lamp. The Boy's body is carried on stage as the actors gather around him. After a call for more light, Chuck turns the lamp away to kick over a chair and free the lamp cord. When he turns the lamp back on the body, it is gone (a quick moving hinged trap which drops the boy actor onto soft mattresses beneath the stage).

Power is restored following a flickering of the lights, and once again we are back in the drab, grey, empty rehearsal stage. The actors are in a state of confusion and panic, searching the theatre for signs of the characters. Gradually, they gather their things and leave the theatre. Only the director (Jeremy) remains, surveying the stage and trying to absorb what he has experienced. Unexpectedly, once again, the scrim begins to tremble and the loading door begins to rise. We see the six characters again, brilliantly back lit, with snatches of their speeches heard over the loudspeakers. Suddenly, all six fall forward on their faces with a loud thud. It is another illusion—a gigantic Polaroid photograph. Jeremy hisses "Jesus" and runs offstage. Blackout. Houselights up. We did not take a curtain call for the sake of maintaining the illusion we had created, but this is entirely at the discretion of the director and the cast.

Some additional hints in rehearsal: Make certain that you maintain a distinct difference in style between the actors and the characters. The actors should be jaunty, relaxed, colloquial, "modern." The characters should be formal, a little stiff. You might also (as we did) paint their faces and hands with pasty white makeup, adding dark highlights under the eyes, to emphasize their otherworldliness. Don't overdo this or it will look like a horror movie effect. When the Father and Stepdaughter refer to the Author, have them actually talk to him (find a spot in the balcony where he's sitting). The most difficult role in the play is that of the Mother, since she has so little to say and must always be the image of grief. Anna Magnani is a good image for her—a heavy, hollow-eyed if once sensual woman. The clothes of the Father and the Son should be significantly better-tailored than those of the rest of the family which are neat but worn. The actors should wear relaxed street clothes, sneakers, and tee shirts. The voice of the technician in the booth can be recorded—but best to use an actual technician rather than an actor.

The production should make the audience's flesh creep. It's a metaphysical ghost story about the transparent nature of reality.

CHARACTERS

SCOTT, stage manager
ANTHONY, a stagehand
JEREMY, director
KAREN ⎫
CHUCK ⎬ actors
TOMMY ⎪
WILL ⎭
FATHER ⎫
MOTHER ⎪
STEPDAUGHTER ⎬ characters
LITTLE BOY ⎪
LITTLE GIRL ⎪
SON ⎭
EMILIO PAZ, a pimp

Six Characters
in Search of an Author

*When the audience enters, the curtain is up and the
stage is abandoned. The theatre is empty, there is no set on
stage, the house is dark. The audience must have the feeling that it has happened into a theatre where not a performance but a rehearsal is about to take place. Downstage is
a small table with three chairs behind it, their backs to the
audience. Houselights are up. A stagehand (Anthony)
wanders onto the stage from the shop in work clothes. Having brought in the backdrop of a set, he is trying to pull
out its wrinkles. The stage manager (Scott) walks on
through the house doors, carrying a coffee pot and a
script. He and Scott exchange hellos.*

SCOTT: After you sweep up, can you get out the Deramo and Smeraldina masks?

ANTHONY: Sure.

SCOTT: Thanks. We're going to need them tonight.
Floyd, you up there? *(calling to the electrician in the
booth who answers through the speaker, "Yeah, Scott")*
Set up something we can use for the *The King
Stag*—you know how Jeremy hates work lights.
(Floyd: "Okay, sure.")

*(The stagehand picks up his tools and materials and
starts sweeping. The actors wander in through the various doors of the theatre, one after the other—Will,
Tommy, and Karen [later, Chuck]—to rehearse Gozzi's*
The King Stag. *As they enter, they improvise greetings
to the stage manager ["Hi, Scott." "Do you need me
right away? I'd like to get a sandwich." "There's a poker
game at Bob's house after rehearsal," etc.] Some sit on*

13

chairs and read the paper; Will lies on the floor and does yoga exercises, waiting for Jeremy [the director] to arrive and start rehearsals. Tommy discusses with Scott where he exits in the scene to be rehearsed, and tries on bits of costume. Jeremy enters through the house doors left.)

SCOTT: All right, settle, everybody. The senior actor's arrived.

(The actors grow quiet and peer into the darkened auditorium. A voice from the back of the theatre calls out, "Hi, chaps." Jeremy, the senior actor, walks down the aisle onto the stage and greets the actors who respond, "How's it going, Jeremy?" To Scott he says, "How you feeling?" Scott: "Not bad.")

JEREMY: What am I supposed to be doing tonight?

SCOTT: *King Stag.* We have to plug Karen into the scene with Deramo in Act 1. I want to make sure they're both comfortable with the movement.

JEREMY: Movement? That's not my job. That's the director's job. I'm just the actor who's coming in to help. That's Andrei Serban's job. He's the director. . . .

SCOTT: You know how busy Andrei is. He's been on the West Coast and back and forth to Europe.

JEREMY: Andrei's never here when he's wanted. He's always farting off all over the world, directing Chekhov in Tokyo, or opera in Cardiff, or no doubt doing something in Greek in Buda-bloody-pest. . . .

KAREN: Oh come on, Jeremy, you've just got your knickers in a twist.

JEREMY: I have not got my knickers in a twist. . . .

14

SCOTT: Let's get going.

JEREMY: It always falls to me. Why is it always me, me, me?

SCOTT: Jeremy, we have done this show three hundred times in eleven different countries—why are you so grouchy tonight?

JEREMY: I am not grouchy. I'm in a very good mood, thank you. And could we have some decent lights for Christ's sake? These new contacts are killing my eyes.

SCOTT: *(to booth)* Floyd, when you're set up could you punch that in, please? Thank you. And kill the house and works. *(In a few seconds, the stage where the actors are standing is lit with a brilliant white light. Scott and Jeremy sit down at the table.)* Thank you.

JEREMY: Oh, that's much better. That's nice and cozy. I like that. So, are we all here?

SCOTT: Chuck's late.

JEREMY: Chuck's late. *(looking at his watch)* I suppose he's plugged into his Walkman somewhere listening to some sports spectacular. Are those wonderful Celtics . . . *(he pronounces this Keltics and is corrected)*. *(Chuck enters, with Walkman headphones over his ears)* All right, let's go then. Oh—who's that roaming in the gloom?

SCOTT: Chuck, five minutes late. . . .

CHUCK: Sorry, everybody. I had to put in a call to Kathy and Jesse.

TOMMY: Why did that take so long?

CHUCK: Rotary. *(dialing)*

WILL: What are you listening to?

15

CHUCK: World Cup soccer. What are we doing?

SCOTT: Act 1, Scene 9, the Smeraldina interview. You've just exited up left. *(Chuck exits up left)*

JEREMY: Will, could you get the other way up, please? It's easier for acting on the whole . . . or possibly not in your case. Okay, let's go. As Scott said, we've done this old chestnut hundreds of times, so let's blow off the cobwebs, give it some energy, and GO.

TOMMY: Jeremy, can I cut down the movement in this scene? It's hard to see with the mask, and it feels dangerous with all that movement.

JEREMY: Don't talk to me, talk to Andrei Serban. He's the director, and you can break your bloody neck as far as he's concerned. It's his favorite bit. You have to realize you're not just moving in this scene, you're representing the spirit of movement. You may not know it, the audience may not know it, the critics may not know it, but Serban knows it. That's enough. *(shouts at Tommy)* You're a metaphor! You have to be symbolic of the thing you're representing. I don't know why this theatre always has to be so bloody different. Why can't we do stuff people like—like *A Christmas Carol*. No, we're always expected to screw up the classics and infuriate the audience and irritate the critics. We can't even do Gozzi straight. Anyhow, in this scene, Deramo is the symbol of innocence and Smeraldina is the symbol of chicanery. Do you understand?

EVERYBODY: No.

JEREMY: Nor do I. Let's go.

SCOTT: Okay. Stand by onstage . . . and GO.

16

(Tommy and Karen take their places. After Tommy jokingly calls "Line," they begin to do a scene from King Stag.*)*

KAREN: My lionhearted lord, in Lombardy we were a family of consequence. Then catastrophes and calamities fell upon us. Dishonest servants stole our wealth, our lands, my jewels. But they could not steal my—hee, hee, hee, modesty. And poverty cannot pollute a noble mind, can it?

TOMMY: So, lady from Lombardy. You love me?

KAREN: Ah, cruel tyrant, can you ask such a question? When already I am utterly yours?

TOMMY: Tell me, Smeraldina, what if I chose you for my wife . . . and then I died, leaving you a widow? Would that make you sad?

(The drop begins to billow as if in a wind. Chuck, who has been awaiting a cue offstage, comes from behind the drop to whisper in Scott's ear. The drop goes transparent, showing six figures upstage in the loading door, backlit by a brilliant light, undulating.)

SCOTT: Hold, please. *(the actors stop)*

JEREMY: Did someone turn on the air conditioning? It's freezing in here.

SCOTT: Jeremy, we'll have to stop for a minute.

JEREMY: What's the matter?

SCOTT: Chuck says some people have come in. He tried to tell them we're working, but they insist on talking to us.

JEREMY: Don't worry, I'll get rid of them. I'll do it. I'll be very diplomatic. I'll ask them to leave in no uncertain terms. *(he walks into the drop)* Anthony,

17

could you take this drop out, please? *(Anthony: "Sure, Jay.")* I nearly ran into it. *(gestures to Scott)* Scott?

SCOTT: Thanks a lot. *(to the Characters)* I'm sorry, but this is a closed rehearsal. Can I ask what you want?

FATHER: *(comes forward, followed by the others, to the foot of the stage)* We're looking for an author.

WILL: So are we. *(laughter)*

FATHER: Any author will do, sir.

JEREMY: Well, we're here rehearsing some classics. We don't have any spare live authors around. Unless you'd like us to resurrect Carlo Gozzi? *(the actors laugh)*

STEPDAUGHTER: *(excitedly, as she rushes forward)* But that's perfect. You have no new plays. We could be the hit of your season.

(A moment to describe the Characters. They are bewildered and ill at ease. These Characters must be completely different from the actors in the company. They are bathed, for example, in their own special light, which follows them everywhere. The Characters are not ghosts but created realities, proceeding from the heat-oppressed imagination, and therefore, Pirandello says, "more real and consistent than the amorphous realities of the actors." The Mother is the picture of sorrow, whose tears seem to have frozen in the corner of her eyes. She is dressed in plain material, with stiff pleats, making it [and her] look as if it were carved.

The Father is about fifty. He has reddish thinning hair, but he is not bald. He has a full mustache and an uncertain, rather vacuous smile. He is pale, with a high forehead. His eyes are blue and oval-shaped, clear

18

and sharp. He wears light trousers and a dark jacket. His voice is rich but at times harsh and strident.

The Mother seems to be crushed under a heavy burden of shame and humiliation. She is wearing a thick black veil and a simple black dress. When she raises the veil, she shows a face like wax, her eyes humbly fixed on the floor.

The Stepdaughter, eighteen years old, is defiant, at times insolent. She is very beautiful, even in her mourning dress, and very elegant. She is disdainful of the timid, suffering, depressed air of her young brother, a scruffy Little Boy of fourteen, who is also dressed in black. But she is full of warmth and tenderness toward her sister, a four-year-old Little Girl who is dressed in white with a black silk sash around her waist.

The Son is twenty-two, tall, frigid, scornful of the Father and indifferent toward the Mother. He wears a massive overcoat and a long green scarf.)

KAREN: This rehearsal has been screwed up enough already.

TOMMY: No more schedule changes, please. We have enough of them.

WILL: I'm having enough trouble remembering my lines for *King Stag!*

CHUCK: I'm sorry, Equity doesn't allow visitors during rehearsals.

FATHER: *(to the Stepdaughter)* I guess there's no author here . . . *(to Jeremy)* unless, maybe, you would like to . . .

KAREN: Are you tourists here?

JEREMY: If you're looking for the Freedom Trail, it's . . . is this supposed to be a joke?

19

FATHER: Of course not! We are bringing you a story of deep anguish.

STEPDAUGHTER: We could put your theatre on the map.

JEREMY: 'Bye now. We wish you luck with all your endeavors, whatever they may be. We're a professional theatre, we're already on the map, and we have work to do. We have no time to waste on tourists. . . . Scott?

FATHER: *(hurt but gentle)* If you *are* a man of the theatre, then you know that life is full of strange things—things that are real, no matter how absurd they seem, and therefore don't need to be pretended.

JEREMY: First you interrupt our rehearsal, and now you insult us. Would you please leave?

FATHER: All I am saying is that it's a little crazy to try to reverse the order of life: to create scenes that are obviously untrue, and then try to convince us they are real. But then I suppose that kind of madness is built into your profession. *(the actors are growing angry)*

KAREN: Somebody else who thinks actors are loonies. Jeremy, can we please get rid of these people?

FATHER: Well, nobody is forcing you to make the false look true. You do it as a game. . . . Isn't it your job on stage to give life to fictional characters?

JEREMY: Look, sir, we do not do it as a game, as you call it. We are professional actors. I'll have you know that the actor's profession is the noblest in the world. *(to Tommy who looks dubious)* Well, it's a living. Even when our playwrights give us bad

20

plays to perform, writing puppets instead of characters, we actors still manage to bring life to the
scripts, right here on this stage, which I wish to
hell you'd get off. . . . *(The actors heartily agree with
Jeremy. "Right on, Jeremy." "You tell them, SA.")*

FATHER: *(bearing in hard with his argument)* There! You
see what I mean? You say you've given life, you've
created characters who are more alive than those
who breathe fresh air and wear street clothes!
Well, perhaps they're not as real, but they're
closer to the truth. We're really in agreement.

CHUCK: Hey, wait a minute. Just before you said . . .

FATHER: Excuse me, but what I said before—about
acting being a game—I said that because you said
you had no time to waste on . . . "tourists"—was
that your word? But who knows better than you
actors that nature uses the human imagination to
create an even more intense reality.

CHUCK: Why are we listening to him? Where is all
this getting us?

FATHER: Nowhere. I'm trying to prove that one can
be thrust into life in a variety of ways and in many
forms—as a tree, as a stone, as water, as a butterfly, perhaps as a woman. And maybe even as a
character in a play.

TOMMY: All right, now let me get this straight. You're
trying to tell us that you were all "thrust into life"
as characters in a play?

FATHER: Exactly! And we're alive, as you can see.

JEREMY: Yes, like a stone, or a butterfly, a stoned butterfly. *(Jeremy and all the actors laugh)*

FATHER: I'm really sorry you think that's funny, because as I told you we are bearing in us a story of

21

great pain and anguish—as you might have guessed from this woman dressed in black. *(at this point he brings the six down slowly to center stage, with tragic elegance, where they are lit by a fantastic bright light)*

CHUCK: Nice lighting, Floyd. Could you save the special effects for us?

FLOYD'S VOICE: *(from booth)* I didn't do anything.

JEREMY: Don't encourage them, Chuck. *(to actors)* Very good pain and anguish. *(turns to the Characters)* And you lot, will you kindly leave the theatre? *(to the stage manager)* Scott, will you call the campus police?

SCOTT: *(comes forward but stops short as if held by a strange force)* This is a private rehearsal. Please leave the theatre.

FATHER: *(to Jeremy)* No, no, I beg you, don't you see . . .

JEREMY: Don't you understand we have work to do?

WILL: *(mumbling)* This would never happen at the Huntingdon.

FATHER: *(coming forward with resolve)* I'm really surprised at you. Why can't you believe me? I guess you've never seen characters who have been created by an author assume real life on a stage face to face with each other. Is it because we haven't given you a written script?

STEPDAUGHTER: *(coming down to Jeremy, smiling and seductive)* We really are six of the most fascinating characters you'll ever meet. But we've been abandoned.

FATHER: That's right, abandoned. The author who first conceived us decided for some reason not to complete the written play and send us into the world of art. That really is a crime, sir, because a fictional character can laugh even in the teeth of death. An invented character is immortal! Men will die. Writers will die! But whatever has been created will live forever. Was there ever a real Sancho Panza or your Sir John Falstaff? But they will live forever because they had the luck to be invented by great imaginative artists.

TOMMY: Excuse me, are you a drama professor on some sort of weird field trip with your group? I mean, what do you want here?

FATHER: We want to live!

TOMMY: Forever, I suppose.

FATHER: No, only for a few moments—through you!

KAREN: What do you mean—live through us?

WILL: That's no way to make a living.

CHUCK: *(pointing to the Stepdaughter)* I wouldn't mind living a little with that chick in the high heels.

FATHER: Listen, our play is all ready to be pasted together. If you actors would help, we could make it all happen.

JEREMY: Excuse me, but I don't understand what you want from us. We don't do improvisations here. We do plays, scripts.

FATHER: That's why we're here.

JEREMY: But where's the script?

FATHER: In us, sir. *(the actors laugh)* The play exists in us. We are the play. And that is why we're in such a passion to show it to you.

STEPDAUGHTER: *(scornfully, but tantalizing and seductive and impudent)* Passion, is it? This is about passion, all right. My passion! For him! *(points to the Father and pretends she is going to embrace him, then stops and breaks into high-pitched laughter)*

FATHER: *(angry)* Stay out of this, will you? And stop laughing at me like that!

STEPDAUGHTER: Ladies and gentlemen, my own father's been dead only two months now. But if you'll give me a chance, I'll show you there's still life left in this little girl. *(sings and dances "My Heart Belongs to Daddy" with suggestive looks at the Father, flirting a little with Chuck, who says, "I'm in love"; the actors applaud heartily)*

CHUCK: Karen, I think she's really got something.

KAREN: Yeah, be careful you don't catch it, Chuck.

SCOTT: What is this, Jay, some kind of audition?

JEREMY: I don't know . . . it's like her version of *Rent* . . . *(to the Father)* Excuse me, sir, but is she . . . uh . . . has she got a little problem?

FATHER: No, it's worse than that.

STEPDAUGHTER: *(to Jeremy)* You bet your life it's worse. Listen, please do this play now! Then you'll see, at the crucial moment when I—when this sweet little girl here—*(taking the Little Girl by the hand away from her Mother and crossing with her to Jeremy)*. Isn't she lovely? *(holds her in her arms)* My sweet, sweet darling! *(lets go of her, very deeply moved almost*

24

against her will) Well, when God takes this lovely little girl away from her poor mother, and this young imbecile *(taking the Little Boy roughly by the sleeve)*, like the idiot he is, does the stupidest thing—oh then you'll see me take off! Yes, run away! But not quite yet, not yet! Because after the things, the intimate things, that have happened between you and me *(pointing to the Father, with a suggestive leer)*, I can't stay with them any more and watch this woman being humiliated by that stuck-up character there *(pointing to the Son)*. Look at him! Just look at him! Patronizing, aloof, because he's the legitimate one! Him! Contemptuous of me, of that boy, of that little girl—because we're bastards. Now you know! Bastards! *(embracing the Mother)* And you won't even acknowledge your own mother—the mother of us all. He looks down on her like she was nothing more than the mother of bastards. The son of a bitch! *(she speaks this rapidly with great excitement, raising her voice on "bastards," and half spitting out "son of a bitch")*

MOTHER: *(with deep anguish, to Jeremy)* Sir, I am begging you, in the name of these two little children ... *(grows faint)* Oh my God ...

FATHER: *(rushing to support her, as the actors grow more bewildered)* Get a chair someone. . . . Quick, a chair for this poor widow.

TOMMY: Has she really fainted?

CHUCK: What's going on here?

FATHER: Look at her! Please look at her!

MOTHER: No! Stop! Please!

FATHER: Let them look at you.

MOTHER: *(lifting her hands and covering her face in shame)* Please, I beg of you, stop this man from doing what he is trying to do. I can't stand it.

WILL: This is getting way beyond me.

JEREMY: Excuse me, sir, but are you two married?

FATHER: Yes, she's my wife.

KAREN: But you just said she's a widow—and you still look pretty lively to me, daddy. *(the bewildered actors find relief in loud laughter and sniggers)*

FATHER: *(wounded and resentful)* Please don't laugh. Stop laughing at us! You see, that's her drama. She had a lover. A man who should be here with us.

MOTHER: No! Stop!

STEPDAUGHTER: He's dead—lucky for him. Died two months ago, like I told you. That's why we're wearing black.

FATHER: Yes, he's dead. But that's not the reason he's not here. He's not here because—well, just take a look at her and you'll understand—we're not talking about a passionate love triangle. She's incapable of love, she can't feel a thing, except maybe a little gratitude—and not for me, for *him*. She's not a woman; she's a mother, that's all. And her drama—you've got to believe me, it's a powerful piece of theatre—her drama is totally involved with these four children she's had by two different men.

MOTHER: Did I want two different men? I didn't choose to have them! It was *his* choice. He forced that other man on me. He *made* me go away with him.

26

STEPDAUGHTER: *(leaping up in anger)* Not true!

MOTHER: Why isn't it true?

STEPDAUGHTER: It isn't. That's all.

MOTHER: You don't know anything about it.

STEPDAUGHTER: It's just not true. *(to Jeremy)* Don't believe a word of it. Do you know why she's lying? Because of him there. *(pointing to the Son)* She tortures herself, wears herself out, and all because of his indifference. She wants him to think that she abandoned him when he was two years old because this man forced her to.

MOTHER: *(passionately)* But he did! He made me do it! I swear to God! *(to Jeremy)* Ask him yourself. *(pointing to the Father)* Make him tell our son the truth. *(to the Stepdaughter)* You know nothing about it.

STEPDAUGHTER: I know how happy you were when my father was alive. Can you deny that?

MOTHER: *(with reluctance)* No.

STEPDAUGHTER: He always loved you deeply. *(to the Little Boy with anger)* Isn't that right? Admit it. Why don't you say something, idiot?

MOTHER: Leave him alone, poor thing. You're trying to make me look ungrateful. You're my daughter. I respect your father's memory. It was not my fault, it was not to please myself that I left his house, left my son.

FATHER: She's right. It was entirely my fault.

CHUCK: If they can't get their story straight, how do they expect anybody else to understand it?

27

KAREN: The whole thing seems a little melodramatic to me.

TOMMY: I think I heard it somewhere before.

JEREMY: *(getting interested)* Look, fellows, could you cool it? I'm interested in this. Do go on. *(he removes himself from the table and goes into the auditorium as if to see how the scene would look from the audience's point of view)*

SON: *(coldly, ironically)* Look at him. Next he'll start spouting philosophy. Soon he'll be telling us all about the Daemon of Experiment.

FATHER: You're a cynical little bastard. *(to Jeremy in the auditorium)* I use a phrase to explain my actions, and you sneer at it.

SON: Words, words, words.

FATHER: Yes, words, words. What else do we have for comfort when we're confused and consumed by guilty thoughts.

STEPDAUGHTER: You just want to bury your guilt, that's all.

FATHER: Bury my guilt? No, that's not true. It would take a lot more than words to do that.

STEPDAUGHTER: Yes, it would take a little cash, too. The money you were going to pay me. *(the actors sense something squalid coming)*

SON: *(contemptuously)* You are disgusting.

STEPDAUGHTER: Am I? What was in that pale blue envelope on the little mahogany table in the room behind Emilio Paz's strip joint? Ah, that name rings a bell, doesn't it? Emilio Paz, king of the grind houses, always happy to help his topless beauties collect a little extra money on the side.

SON: And she thinks she now has the right to abuse our whole family just because he was going to give her that money. But as it turned out, the transaction never took place.

STEPDAUGHTER: We came awfully close.

MOTHER: Stop, daughter. You ought to be ashamed of yourself.

STEPDAUGHTER: I don't feel shame, what I feel is an overwhelming desire for revenge. I'm dying, dying to play that scene! The little room. I can see it clearly. The girls leave their street clothes over there, there's the convertible couch, there's the mirror, there's the Chinese screen, and right there in front of the window is the little mahogany table with the pale blue envelope on it. It's absolutely real. I could pick it up now! But don't anybody look, because I'm almost naked! No shame, no blushes—I leave that to him. *(pointing to the Father)* He was pretty shaky then, I can tell you that.

WILL: Does anyone understand what the hell's going on?

FATHER: I don't blame you for being confused when all you hear is her side! Why don't you give me a chance to reply to these horrible slanders?

STEPDAUGHTER: Nobody wants to listen to your long-winded excuses.

FATHER: No excuses! I want to explain the facts.

STEPDAUGHTER: Yes, your facts.

FATHER: We can never understand each other. For example, all the pity and compassion I felt for this woman *(the Mother)*, she still believes is only vengeance and hatred.

MOTHER: But you kicked me out of the house.

FATHER: You see? I kicked her out! She actually believes that!

MOTHER: I can't talk as good as you, I'm not educated enough. . . . But believe me, sir, *(to Jeremy)* after we got married . . . I don't know why he married me, a poor uneducated woman.

FATHER: But that's why I married you—because you were simple. That's what I loved about you, I . . . *(exasperated over his failure to make her understand, he throws up his hands)* Do you see the problem? She simply can't . . . it's maddening, maddening, this mental deafness of hers. She can feel love for her children, yes, but up here *(taps his forehead)* deaf, infuriatingly deaf.

STEPDAUGHTER: Yes, but ask him to explain what good all his intelligence has done for us.

FATHER: If we only knew what misery comes from our efforts to do good.

KAREN: Excuse me, but, Jeremy, can we please go on with our rehearsal?

TOMMY: I'm sure I heard it somewhere before.

KAREN: Yeah, they were guests on the Jenny Jones Show.

JEREMY: *(to the Father)* Sir, you've obviously got an interesting story here, but we were rehearsing a play when you came in here, and we really can't spend all our rehearsal time on this. Do you think

30

you can tell your story more clearly? We'll give you ten minutes. *(to the others)* Is that all right, ten minutes? *(the actors reluctantly give assent)*

SCOTT: All right, ten minutes, and I'm going to time this.

FATHER: All right. You see, there was a fellow working as my assistant—quite poor, very loyal, devoted to her *(pointing to Mother)*. Nothing underhand, you must believe that. He was a good, simple person . . . like her. Neither thought for a moment they were doing anything wrong.

STEPDAUGHTER: So he thought it for them.

FATHER: Not true! What I did, I did for her—yes, for me too, I admit it. It got to a point where I couldn't say a thing without one of them shooting the other a secret look—they seemed to be asking each other how to react to what I said, how to avoid irritating me. This made me angrier. I was always angry.

JEREMY: So why didn't you fire the poor bastard?

FATHER: I did, finally. But then I had to watch this unhappy woman moping around the house, like a stray dog looking for a place to lie down.

MOTHER: That's true.

FATHER: *(suddenly, turning as if to stop her)* And is it also true about the boy?

MOTHER: He tore my own son from my arms, when he was only a baby.

FATHER: But not out of cruelty. I only wanted him to grow up strong and healthy, in touch with the earth.

31

STEPDAUGHTER: *(pointing to the Son, jeering)* And what a magnificent success you've achieved.

FATHER: Is it my fault he turned out this way? I took him to a wet nurse in the country because his mother didn't seem strong enough. Also a peasant woman, like her. Simple women attract me— maybe that's wrong, but I've always felt the need for a kind of sound moral cleanliness. *(the Stepdaughter breaks out in raucous laughter)* Please make her stop that. It's awful.

JEREMY: Do shut up, will you? How can I follow the story if you make that awful racket? I'm sorry, sir, do go on. *(After Jeremy rebukes her, the Stepdaughter assumes her usual position . . . absorbed and distant, half smiling. Jeremy again checks out the scene from the auditorium.)*

FATHER: I couldn't bear to have this woman near me. *(pointing to the Mother)* Not because she had upset me, and not because she suffocated me, but because I felt so terribly sorry for her.

MOTHER: And so he sent me away.

FATHER: *(defensive)* You were well provided for. Yes, I sent her away to the other man, so she could be free of me.

MOTHER: So *you* could be free.

FATHER: Yes, that's partly true. But I did it more for her, I swear it. *(folds his arms, then turns suddenly to the Mother)* I kept a close eye on you, didn't I? Until one day that fellow suddenly took her away to another city, resenting my interest in them. Until then I watched this new little family grow up; first this girl, then the others. I felt very ten-der toward them. She'll tell you that. *(points to the Stepdaughter)*

STEPDAUGHTER: Oh yes indeed. I was a cute little thing, you know, with hair down to my waist and frilly little underwear. He used to watch me coming out of school. He came to see how I was filling out.

FATHER: That's a lie! A vicious lie!

STEPDAUGHTER: It's the truth.

FATHER: Vicious! Vicious! *(he continues)* After she'd gone, my home was empty. She'd been a heavy weight on me, but her presence filled the house. I wandered through the empty rooms like a damned soul. This boy here *(to the Son)* was raised and educated away from home. When he came back—I don't know—he didn't seem mine any more, without a mother to link us together. Anyway, he grew away from me; we had no connection through love or anything. I wanted to fill the emptiness of my life. And so I thought more and more about them, that other family, wrapped up in their simple cares, free of my intellectual complications. And that's why I used to watch that child coming out of school.

STEPDAUGHTER: Will you listen to him? He used to *follow* me down the street, smiling at me and waving his hand! I watched him, wide-eyed, puzzled. Who was he? I asked my mother about him. *(going to Mother and putting head on her lap, a little child again)* Mama? She knew. *(Mother nods)* She kept me out of school for a few days. When I went back *(again a little girl)*, there he was again—a sad-looking figure, holding a brown paper bag. He came nearer and stroked me. In the bag

33

(excited) . . . was a beautiful silk shawl with a fringe on it. All for me?

JEREMY: Sorry, this is all fascinating, but dramatically it's irrelevant.

SON: *(contemptuously)* Yes, just literature.

FATHER: What do you mean, literature? This is life, my boy, real emotions.

JEREMY: That may be! But it won't work in the theatre.

FATHER: I know it won't. But this is only the background of the action. You don't put this on stage. As you can see, she isn't a little girl any more with long hair down to her waist.

STEPDAUGHTER: —or with frilly little underwear showing under her dress.

FATHER: The real drama begins now. And I can assure you, it's new and innovative.

STEPDAUGHTER: *(coming forward, fierce and brooding)* When my father died . . .

FATHER: They came back here. Only I didn't know it. I had lost touch with them over the years. The drama was about to break out, violent and unexpected. I hadn't learned how to do without sex. I was lonely but revolted by casual affairs—not old enough to do without women, not young enough to have them without feeling disgust. Ashamed of myself but unable to suppress my desires. What good was my intelligence? And the women—what about them? You find one who looks at you warmly. You hold her in your arms. And the next thing she does is close her eyes. She's telling the man: "Blind yourself, for I am blind."

34

STEPDAUGHTER: And if she doesn't close her eyes, what then? When she looks directly into the sweating face of a man who comes to her without love, what then? Oh what disgust she feels for this attempt to justify lust, excuse it. . . . I can't listen to this shit any more. His intellectualizing is contemptible. He makes me sick.

CHUCK: *(from under the earphones)* Can we get to the point at last? I'd like to listen to the playoffs. *(or "I can feel my hair falling out")*

FATHER: All right, then. But I'm just trying to provide you with some motivation. Isn't that what you actors always want? Anyway, how was I to know that they had all come back here after that poor fellow died, that they were dreadfully poor, and that the mother had gone to work as a dressmaker, sewing costumes for Emilio Paz, of all people.

MOTHER: Believe me, I had no way of knowing that man gave me work because he had his eye on my daughter. . . .

STEPDAUGHTER: Poor Mama. Do you know what that pimp would say when I brought back the stuff you'd been working on? That you didn't know how to sew a sequin, that you were messing up the seams. So you see, I had to find ways to bring in more cash while you sat home all night, thinking you were sacrificing yourself for me and these two children, sewing away at bras and G-strings for Emilio Paz.

WILL: And it was in the strip joint that you met . . . ?

STEPDAUGHTER: *(pointing to the Father)* Him. Oh, he was an old customer there. What a scene that's going to be . . . terrific!

FATHER: With her, the mother, coming in . . .

STEPDAUGHTER: *(quickly, savagely)* Almost in time!

FATHER: *(crying out)* No, *just* in time, *just* in time. Luckily I found out who she was before it was too late. I took all of them back to my house then. Try to imagine that scene, with the two of us living in the same house. She behaving . . . just like she does here; and I unable to look her in the face.

STEPDAUGHTER: God, it's so ridiculous. After what happened at Emilio Paz's, do you think it's possible for me to behave like a sweet young thing, modest and virtuous, in order to justify your pretentious notions about "sound moral cleanliness"?

FATHER: That's what's so interesting to me about life and drama, the way we tend to think of ourselves as a single personality. But it's not true. Each of us is many different complex people, and all of those people live inside of us. We discover this when we suddenly find ourselves doing something that defines us, and we hang there, as if in chains, summed up, for all time, by a single action. Now do you understand how this girl betrayed me? By accident she found me in a place I had no right to be, doing something I had no right to do. And now she wants to fix me in a reality that is alien to my nature, that came from a single uncharacteristic action of my life. That is what really hurts. You'll see what a tremendous impact the play will have when this theme of mine becomes clear. But other positions have to be considered. His . . . *(pointing to the Son)*

SON: *(with a scornful shrug)* Leave me out of it. This has nothing to do with me.

36

FATHER: Why not?

SON: I'm not involved, and I don't want to be involved. You know perfectly well I was never supposed to get mixed up with you all.

STEPDAUGHTER: We're vulgar and common, you see! And he's so high class! But you may have noticed that whenever I look at this well-bred member of the upper crust, he can't face me directly. . . . He knows what he's done to me.

SON: *(not looking at her)* Me?

STEPDAUGHTER: Yes, you. Whose fault is it, sweetheart, that I went back to peddling my ass? Yours! *(the actors start at this)* Didn't you make us feel like strangers in your home, intruding on your legitimate kingdom? He says I acted like a tyrannical bitch, but look how he treated us. According to him, we had no right to move into his house with my mother—but she's his mother too.

SON: Look how they're ganging up on me. But consider my point of view. One day I'm sitting home quietly when this creature, acting as if she owns the place, comes in and asks for my father. God knows what business she has with him. The next minute, with the same bold look in her eye, she comes back with that little girl there. And she begins to treat my father, I don't know why, in the most suggestive and forward way—demanding money from him as if he owed it to her.

FATHER: In a way, I did. I owed it to your mother.

SON: My mother? How was I supposed to know that? I had never seen her before. I had never even heard her name mentioned. Anyway, one day she comes in with her *(pointing to the Stepdaughter)* and with the little boy and that little girl. And they say to me, *(Stepdaughter speaks)* "Don't you know this is your mother, too?" *(Son continues)* Little by little I begin to understand. But I'm out of it. Believe me, I'm an undeveloped dramatic character, and I'm very uncomfortable in their company. So please leave me out of it.

FATHER: But it's because of your feelings that . . .

SON: *(exasperated)* What do you know about my feelings? When have you ever shown the slightest interest in my feelings?

FATHER: Yes, I admit that's true. But this coldness of yours, this withdrawal, it's cruel to me and it's criminal to your mother. When she came back to the house and saw you for the first time, imagine what she felt knowing you were her son but not being able to recognize you. . . . *(points out the Mother to the actors)* There, look, she's crying.

STEPDAUGHTER: *(angrily)* Damned fool.

FATHER: *(turning toward the Son)* He says he's out of it, but he's really the crux of the action. Look at this little boy here, who's always hanging on to this mother, scared, humiliated. And all because of that one there! Maybe this little boy has the biggest problem of all. He feels like the real outsider, more than the others. He feels so ashamed, so humiliated, just being in the house. He feels like a charity case, you see. *(quietly)* Just like his father—shy, quiet, reserved.

WILL: *(W. C. Fields voice)* Never get on the stage with kids or dogs.

FATHER: He won't be on stage long. Neither will the little girl—she's the first to go.

JEREMY: Look, sir, I have to admit, you've got me. Your story is fascinating—quite fascinating. I think it's got the makings of a good play.

STEPDAUGHTER: *(trying to push in)* Especially when it features a character like me.

FATHER: *(pushing her away, wanting to hear what Jeremy has to say)* Just stay out of it!

JEREMY: *(ignoring the interruption)* And if nothing else, it's original.

FATHER: Oh, absolutely original! I told you so.

JEREMY: But you must admit it was awfully pushy the way you barged your way in here.

FATHER: I'm sure you understand. We see a stage and we can't stay away from it.

TOMMY: You're actors, are you? Where—in community theatre?

FATHER: No, no, we're attracted to the stage because . . .

JEREMY: Tommy, I think they may be pros. They handle themselves very well.

FATHER: *(angrily)* I'm not an actor.

TOMMY: Sorry.

FATHER: *(back in control)* No, like most people I can only act the part I've chosen for myself, or that's been chosen for me. But as you see, the role sometimes runs away from me, and I get a little melodramatic. All of us do.

JEREMY: Yes, I have heard that said. The story is fascinating, but as a play it needs polishing; it needs a playwright. I can give you the names and addresses of some agents . . .

FATHER: No, no. Look, here's the thing. Why doesn't your company do it?

KAREN: Us? What's he talking about?

FATHER: Yes, you. Why not?

CHUCK: But none of us have ever written anything. Jeremy wrote something once, but they wouldn't even do it on TV.

FATHER: Why not start now? It's simple. And it'll be easier for you, because all the characters are right here, alive in front of your eyes.

JEREMY: That's not enough.

FATHER: But why not? After you've seen us live out our drama . . .

JEREMY: We still need someone to write it.

FATHER: Write it *down*, you mean. Because it's going to happen right in front of you, live, in color, scene by scene, line by line. All you have to do is sketch it out and then it's performed.

TOMMY: Jeremy, this may sound crazy, but I think they've got the makings of a very good play here. There's plenty of time to plug Karen into *King Stag*. Why don't we use the rest of this evening to try it out?

JEREMY: It's tempting. It just might work.

FATHER: It *will* work. Wait till you see what great things come out of it. I can give you a scene breakdown right now.

JEREMY: I'm tempted, I'm tempted. What do you say, fellows, should we give it a whirl? *(the actors are more or less in agreement, except for Chuck who shouts "No!")* All right, come into the green room and we'll copy down an outline. *(to Chuck)* I can't concentrate here with all this enthusiasm. Okay, Scott, take a short break.

SCOTT: How long a break, Jeremy?

JEREMY: Oh, just a couple of minutes. *(as Scott calls: "This is not an official break. Just stay here, and no one leave the theatre," Jeremy says to Father)* Let's go. I have a feeling we may be onto something here.

FATHER: Absolutely. Don't you think the others should come too?

JEREMY: Yes, would you people come along. Children, madam, you, sir, kiddies. *(going, he turns to the actors)* I won't be more than a couple of minutes.

(As Jeremy and the six Characters exit, leaving the actors on stage, Will says: "Jeremy, make me the young lover." Jeremy: "We're not doing science fiction.")

CHUCK: Scott, is Jeremy serious about this?

SCOTT: You heard him as well as I did, Chuck.

KAREN: I think he had a little too much Beaujolais at dinner.

TOMMY: I hate to always be Andy Hardy around here, but is it going to kill us to try something new for a change?

WILL: How are we supposed to make up a play in five minutes?

CHUCK: I'm not going to get on stage with six people who walk in off the street.

TOMMY: Would you rather rehearse *King Stag* for the nine millionth time?

WILL: *(screaming)* No!!!!

KAREN: Well, if you put it that way.

WILL: Who the hell are these people?

CHUCK: Escapees from McLean's.

TOMMY: Well, Jeremy is certainly taking them seriously.

CHUCK: Come on—Jeremy thought Mr. Ed was great art.

KAREN: You know, this is like the stuff we used to do at The Next Move . . .

WILL: . . . get in there and work from zero . . .

CHUCK: *(interrupting)* You mean your IQ? I'm going out to the lobby to get a Coke. *(He goes out into the lounge, through the side door. The actors keep talking until Jeremy returns.)*

TOMMY: Get an attitude check.

SCOTT: Anthony, you still awake?

WILL: *(after a pause)* You know, an empty theatre always gives me the spooks. It's like the ghosts of all the shows we've done are somewhere on the stage.

KAREN: And all the characters we've played.

TOMMY: Isn't that what those people were trying to say? Do you think it's possible for a dramatic

42

character to continue to exist after an actor's done playing the part?

WILL: Take it easy, Tommy. All I said was, an empty theatre gives me the spooks.

TOMMY: No, but listen. Isn't that what we try to do when we act—we try to bring life to something that's dead on the page. Now who's to say if when we bring this character to life, you know, this personality, that maybe it does continue to live on in some way. Maybe it does haunt the theatre, you know.

KAREN: If that's the case, there's a lot more male ghosts hanging around this stage than females.

TOMMY: Wouldn't you feel better if you knew something you'd created, that you brought to life, could continue to exist? I mean, in the movies there's a record; but here, on the stage, all we do is rehearse it, perform it, and then it closes and it's gone.

KAREN: Until the next role.

TOMMY: But it's the same way every play.

WILL: Except for *King Stag,* which goes on forever.

TOMMY: Well, that's the exception to the rule.

KAREN: I think I see what Tommy means. All these people are asking is to be taken seriously. Maybe we should give them a chance. What have we got to lose?

WILL: I don't think we have any choice when Jeremy's already decided to do their play.

KAREN: Well, if we have to do it, let's at least have some fun with it.

43

WILL: I'll do it, but don't expect me to enjoy it.

TOMMY: Nobody expects miracles.

KAREN: Scott, where's Jeremy?

JEREMY: *(returning with the Characters)* Okay, Scott, I think we've got something. It's going to be a lot of fun but a lot of hard work.

TOMMY: And we don't have a lot of time.

JEREMY: Let's get going. Is everyone here?

SCOTT: Chuck's in the lobby.

JEREMY: Chuck's in the lobby? Well, we'll go without Chuck. Scott, I'm going to need your help. They want some props, some furniture and some costumes.

SCOTT: Sure, fine.

JEREMY: First they want a sofa.

(Scott makes arrangements with Anthony, who lugs on the required materials. Meanwhile, Chuck, still wearing his headphones, wanders into the house from the side door and is greeted by the other actors, inquiring about the score of the game. Jeremy shoots him an impatient look.)

ANTHONY: What sofa?

SCOTT: You know, that little green sofa in the wings.

STEPDAUGHTER: No, it wasn't green. And it wasn't little. It was a big yellow convertible couch with beer stains on it. It was huge. And very comfortable.

ANTHONY: That sofa went to Zero Church Street, but I did see a bench . . .

44

JEREMY: That'll be perfect. It doesn't matter. Who cares?

STEPDAUGHTER: What do you mean, who cares? That was Emilio Paz's famous balling couch.

JEREMY: I dare say it was, dear, but this is only a rehearsal, so let me do it my way. Now, they want a window piece . . .

SCOTT: I'm sure there are frames left over from something back there.

STEPDAUGHTER: Don't forget that little mahogany table for the blue envelope.

ANTHONY: *(to Jeremy)* Case has a prop table offstage.

JEREMY: Mahogany?

FATHER: We need a mirror.

STEPDAUGHTER: And a screen. I have to have the screen or I can't do the scene.

SCOTT: No problem, we have a folding change screen offstage right.

FATHER: *(insistent)* And a *mirror.*

STEPDAUGHTER: Very important for the customers.

SCOTT: There's a dance mirror in the flies.

JEREMY: But that's huge.

SCOTT: The only other thing we've got is a little makeup mirror.

JEREMY: The dance mirror will have to do. Okay . . . what else do they want . . . they want a clothes rack with some costumes for the strippers.

STEPDAUGHTER: Yes, lots of them, please.

SCOTT: *The King Stag* rack is right offstage. I'll pull some stuff out of stock. What kind of costumes do you want, Jeremy?

JEREMY: I don't know. Whatever it is that strippers wear these days. It's been so long. *(Scott goes off to get the costumes while Anthony sets up the furniture and props for the scene)* Okay, Tommy, here is a breakdown of the play, scene by scene. *(he hands out sheets to the actors)*

TOMMY: Oh great. *(looking at his sheet)* Hey, Will, you're going to love this—no lines to learn.

JEREMY: That's the thing. We're going to take them down as they go along. As they say them. . . . Oh, Scott, have you got a tape recorder?

SCOTT: No, but there's some blank yellow paper on the table. . . .

JEREMY: All right. Tommy, you know speedwriting, don't you? *(Tommy nods)* Okay, we'll write the lines down as they say them. That'll be great.

KAREN: Excuse me, Jeremy, but do you want me to pay more attention to what they're saying or what they're doing?

JEREMY: *(anticipating her)* Well, both actually—what they're saying *and* what they're doing. It'll all be written down, don't worry. You won't have to improvise.

CHUCK: What are we doing?

JEREMY: Oh, Chuck, take off those earphones. *(Chuck: "What?")* Take off those earphones. *(Chuck: "Oh, charades")* No, not charades. This is a rehearsal—and they're the ones *(pointing to the Characters)* who'll do the rehearsing. . . .

46

FATHER: *(bewildered)* Us? I'm sorry, but what do you mean, we rehearse?

JEREMY: I mean you'll be rehearsing for the benefit of the actors.

FATHER: But we are the characters. . . .

JEREMY: That's right. You're the characters. But characters don't do the acting here. The actors do the acting . . . the characters stay where they belong, in the script—when there is a script.

FATHER: That's exactly what I mean. There isn't any script. You're lucky enough to have the actual characters right here in front of you.

TOMMY: Terrific! They want to write it, act in it, direct it . . .

FATHER: But that's what we're here for.

WILL: What do you think we get paid for? The little we do get paid.

CHUCK: I'm an actor, not a member of the audience. *(actually, he is sprawled out in one of the seats)*

JEREMY: You could have fooled me. *(the actors laugh)*

SCOTT: Mirror coming in.

JEREMY: Okay, let's get on with it. First we have to give your wife a name.

FATHER: Emilia.

JEREMY: But isn't that her real name? We can't use her real name.

FATHER: But why not, if that's what she's called? Still, if somebody else is going to play the part . . . I've always thought of her as . . . but it's up to you. *(a little confused)* It's weird . . . I don't know how to describe it. . . . I'm already beginning to feel a little fake. It's like my own words don't belong to me any more.

TOMMY: *(gently)* Don't worry. Every beginning actor feels that. It's stage fright. Just relax, breathe. You'll get over it in a minute.

JEREMY: That's right, don't worry. And if you want to call her Emilia, she'll be Emilia—until we think of a less boring name. Okay, now what? Oh, we've got to cast the play. *(to Tommy)* You can play the Son. And you, *(to Karen)* of course, are perfectly cast as the Stepdaughter.

STEPDAUGHTER: *(excited)* Her? Are you serious? That woman is going to play *me?* *(bursts out laughing)*

JEREMY: Uh-oh . . . *(themes of doom from Tommy)*

KAREN: What the hell is her problem? I don't like being insulted!

STEPDAUGHTER: I'm really sorry. I wasn't really laughing at you.

JEREMY: Karen is a damned fine actress. You should feel proud to be played by . . .

KAREN: *(quickly and scornfully)* . . . that woman!

STEPDAUGHTER: But you're missing my point. It's not her, really. It's me I'm thinking about. I just don't see myself in you . . . you're nothing like me at all.

FATHER: Yes, that's what I'm trying to say too. You see, our reality . . .

JEREMY: What do you mean, your "reality." What is this Method crap? Do you think your "reality"

48

only exists inside you? Do you think you have exclusive rights to what you are? Nonsense.

FATHER: What? Don't we even possess our own reality?

JEREMY: Of course not. You're just raw material here on this stage—basic stuff to which we actors give form and flesh and tone and gesture.

CHUCK: And we've played a lot better characters in a lot better plays than this one.

WILL: Sad stuff. If it works on stage, it'll be because of our company.

FATHER: I don't want to argue with you, but I don't think you get the point. Our story isn't sad or trivial to us. It's making us suffer terribly—now, at this moment, you can see it in our faces, in the way we move our bodies. . . .

TOMMY: Excuse me, sir, but you're forgetting one thing. We're actors. We know how to do that, and the other stuff we can take care of with makeup and costuming.

FATHER: Yes, but our voices, our gestures.

JEREMY: Look, I'm not going to argue any more. If you want us to do your bloody play you simply cannot play yourselves. The actors will play your parts, and that's all there is to it!

TOMMY: Thank you.

FATHER: I'm beginning to understand why our author didn't want to put us on stage. I'm sure your actors are all very gifted; I don't want to hurt their feelings. But if I'm going to be impersonated by . . . by . . . I don't know who . . .

49

WILL: *(rising proudly to the occasion)* By me, sir, if you don't mind.

FATHER: *(with respect)* I'm honored, sir. *(he bows)* But I have to say that no matter how hard this gentleman works to imitate me . . . *(breaks off, confused)*

WILL: *(haughtily)* I'm listening.

FATHER: I mean, even with makeup . . . we don't exactly look alike. *(the actors laugh)* It won't be easy to act me as I really am. It will end up—now, I'm not talking about his size and build—it will end up more as an interpretation of me, *his* idea of me, and not what I know I am. How will that be understood by the people who render judgment on us?

CHUCK: Oh, he's worried about the critics already.

JEREMY: We can't do anything about the critics— they're *our* pain and anguish. We're wasting a lot of time. Let's get going. *(stepping out and looking around; to the Stepdaughter)* Does this all look okay to you?

STEPDAUGHTER: This? I don't recognize a thing.

CHUCK: Christ, does she expect us to reconstruct the whole nine yards?

JEREMY: *(to the Father)* Didn't you say the room behind the bar had wallpaper?

FATHER: Yes. Flowered.

JEREMY: So it's striped wallpaper, for Christ's sake. We're working with available material here. I think we have all the furniture we need. And someone's even turned a fan on so the curtain's going blowy, blowy, blowy. Are we all ready? No. Scott, we need an envelope, pale blue if you have one, and give it to this gentleman here. *(pointing to the Father)*

SCOTT: A business envelope or a letter envelope?

JEREMY and FATHER: A letter envelope.

TOMMY: Want to use my phone bill?

JEREMY: Right then. Let's start. The first scene is the lady's. *(Karen moves forward on stage)* No, not you yet. This lady. *(points to Stepdaughter)* You stay still and watch.

STEPDAUGHTER: *(grandly)* Watch how I bring it . . . to life!

KAREN: *(hurt)* Don't worry, I know how to bring a part . . . to life! And I didn't even go . . . to Yale!

JEREMY: That's very good. The first scene is between this lady and Emilio Paz. Oh! Wait a minute. *(worried, and looking out into the audience)* Where *is* Paz?

FATHER: He isn't here; he's not with us.

JEREMY: So what do we do?

FATHER: But he's real, as real as we are.

JEREMY: Well, if he is, where is he?

FATHER: Can I handle this? *(to the actors)* Would you kindly lend me some clothing? Something flashy—a scarf, or some gloves, some fancy rings. That hat there.

WILL: My hat? What do you need a hat for?

FATHER: I just want to borrow it for a moment.

SCOTT: Sir, what about this shawl?

FATHER: That's perfect.

51

KAREN: Please be careful, it's new. *(Dorchester accent)* That's my Filene's Basement bargain.

FATHER: I just want to hang it up here for a minute. I won't damage it. Do you mind?

KAREN: *(handing her shawl to the Father)* I think this whole thing's crazy. What's this for, to dress the set?

FATHER: Exactly, to dress the set.

JEREMY: I'd like to know exactly what you're doing.

FATHER: I'm trying to dress the set with the kind of things Paz might be familiar with. That way, the place will seem more congenial to him, and, who knows, he might even come and join us. *(quiet and conspiratorial)* Now, everybody, be very quiet. Keep an eye on that mirror up there. Watch. Watch.

(The mirror turns transparent and a shaft of light illuminates the figure of Emilio Paz, standing in the back room of his strip joint where the real furniture—window, couch, clothes rack, mahogany table—parallels the improvised materials in front of the mirror. He is a lithe, well-built man, with long black hair, wearing vulgar clothes without a shirt, pendants hanging from his neck. When discovered, he is taking a sniff of cocaine through a tube. At the sight of this apparition, Jeremy and the actors panic, running off the stage and into the aisles of the house. The Stepdaughter, however, goes upstage to the mirror and greets Paz respectfully.)

STEPDAUGHTER: He's here! He's here!

FATHER: *(smiling broadly)* It's him! I told you he'd come. He's here!

JEREMY: *(recovering from shock, and angry)* Jesus H. Christ, that's some trick!

CHUCK: What the hell's going on here?

TOMMY: Where did they find that other character?

KAREN: They were hiding him in the shop.

WILL: I think they're into magic, sleight of hand. It's a mirror trick.

FATHER: Please. Don't spoil this miracle by explaining it. Don't you see how extraordinary reality is? This man has been brought to life, lured to this spot, reproduced in toto for the sake of this scene—and with more right to live than any of you. There's certainly more reality in him than in you. Which of you actors can improve on Emilio Paz there? *(to Tommy)* You? *(to Will)* You? This is the true Emilio Paz. No actor who plays him can be as genuine, as authentic, as he is in person. You noticed how my daughter recognized him the moment he arrived. Now watch—just watch this scene.

JEREMY: Chuck, take a gander at this. You'll be playing Emilio Paz. *(Chuck: "You bet.")*

(Jeremy and the actors move back to watch. But the scene between the Stepdaughter and Paz has already begun while the actors were protesting and the Father responding. It is being played very quietly, naturalistically, obviously too small for the stage. When the attention of the actors is requested by the Father, they turn to see that the Stepdaughter's image has been projected into Paz's back room. They strain to hear her speak but the words are unintelligible. After listening hard for a few moments, they start to make fun of them.)

53

TOMMY: Do you want me to get this down, Jeremy?

JEREMY: Yeah, please.

WILL: I can't hear a word they're saying.

KAREN: Not a thing.

TOMMY: I can't either, Jeremy. I can't write it if I can't hear it.

CHUCK: Projection, please, projection.

STEPDAUGHTER: *(leaving Paz, who has a mysterious smile on his face, and coming down to the actors)* Projection! What do you mean, "projection"? We can't bellow the sort of things we're talking about. Before it was different—I could shout my shame to embarrass him for the sake of revenge. But this is an entirely different matter. It could mean jail for Paz.

CHUCK: What the hell are you talking about? You're in a theatre, you have to be heard.

TOMMY: I'm practically on the stage with you and I can't hear. What about the audience? They paid good money for this.

JEREMY: Yes, it's a fantastic effect, but we have to think about the audience. We actors have to bring the scene to life. I admit you would speak more quietly if you were alone in that little room, in which case, we wouldn't be around to hear you anyway. But this is a play rehearsal. So just pretend you're all by yourself in that little room behind the bar. *(the Stepdaughter, with a sardonic smile, wags her finger and her head, as if to say no)*

JEREMY: Well, why not?

STEPDAUGHTER: *(mysteriously, in a loud whisper)* Because there's somebody outside who would hear him if he spoke normally.

WILL: You're not planning to materialize anyone else, are you? *(the actors get ready to disappear again)*

FATHER: No, she's talking about me. I should be there, waiting behind the door, and Paz knows I'm waiting. Please excuse me; I have to go get ready to come in. *(he starts to go on stage)*

JEREMY: *(stopping him)* Wait a minute. A little stage decorum. Before you get to that bit, you have to . . .

STEPDAUGHTER: *(interrupting)* Yes, that bit, that bit! Let's do it *now*! I'm dying to do that scene. If he's ready for it, I'm ready.

JEREMY: *(shouting)* No, no, no, no, no, no, NO! Before we get to you and him, we have to do the scene between you and Paz.

STEPDAUGHTER: Oh God! He's just finished telling what you know already, that my mother's sewing is lousy, that she's ruined a costume, and that he's thought of a way to help us out of the whole mess.

PAZ: *(speaking with an air of great importance)* Si, señor, because she is nice little chiquita linda. Nice and tight, make you feel all right. I no want mucho dinero. I am, how you say, un hombre generoso.

WILL: Is this guy an escapee from Taco Bell? *(the actors are laughing)*

TOMMY: What a phony accent. *(also laughing)*

55

PAZ: No me gusto que you gringos laugh at me Inglesa. I spik de Inglesa lo mejor que yo puedo, señor.

JEREMY: No, he's right. Don't laugh at him. This is great. Talk just that way, Señor . . . uh . . . thingy. It'll work fine—a little ethnic humor can't hurt. Can you do this, Chuck? *(Chuck: "Jess, I dink so.")* This is super. Absolutely super.

STEPDAUGHTER: Super? You bet. A pimp with an accent will be very funny, won't it? You'll get a real big laugh when you hear him say there's a viejo señor outside looking for a good time. No es verdad, Emiliano?

PAZ: No esta viejo, pero no es joven. Un señor de cinquenta años. In his golden middle ages. Si no le gusta, eef you do not like him, no se necessario.

(The Mother leaps up, astonishing the actors who have been ignoring her. When she shouts, they are startled and try to restrain her. But she has already aimed a blow at Paz's head with her pocketbook, which sends him reeling.)

MOTHER: You pimp! Pimp! Murderer! Oh, my poor daughter!

STEPDAUGHTER: *(running across to her Mother)* No, mother, please!

FATHER: *(also running across)* Stay calm, stay calm. Come and sit down.

STEPDAUGHTER: *(to Jeremy who has also crossed to her)* My mother can't stand to be in the same room with him.

FATHER: *(also speaking to Jeremy)* They simply can't oc-
cupy the same space. That's why Paz wasn't along
when we first arrived. If they meet too early, the
scene loses its climax.

JEREMY: It's not important! We're only doing a
stumble-through. Everything can be used—even
if it's messy we can clean it up later. *(turning to the
Mother and helping her to a seat)* Come on,
madame, take it easy, take it easy! Sit down for a
while. This is great!

STEPDAUGHTER: Go on, Emilio.

PAZ: *(offended)* Absolutamente no! Las negocias son
impossible con una mujer nerviosa.

STEPDAUGHTER: Let's do it, let's go. Bring in the viejo
señor who wants to have a good time with me.
(turning to the others) You see, this next scene *has*
to be played—we've got to do it now. *(to Paz)* Oh,
leave if you have to.

PAZ: I leave, I leave. No es tranquilo aqui. I am a
man of peaces and quiet. I no stay with gringos
locos. What this woman want? She want to swing
her pocketbook, let her go street. *(he puts his wig
furiously in place, glares at the actors, and bangs out of
the theatre as the actors applaud his exit)*

STEPDAUGHTER: *(to Father)* Now, come on! No, you
don't have to exit again. Come back here! Just
pretend you've already come on. Look, I'm sitting
here modestly with my eyes on the ground—well,
speak up! Use that unctuous little voice of yours:
"Good afternoon, my dear"!

JEREMY: Are you directing this show, peachy pie, or
am I? *(to Father, who looks confused)* Go on, say the
line. Walk upstage—no, don't bother to make an-

other entrance. Then take a few steps downstage again. That's right.

(The Father does as he is told, almost hypnotically. He is very pale, already deeply immersed in the reality of his recreated life. He smiles as he nears the stage, almost as if unaware of the drama that is about to take place. The actors watch intently the scene that is beginning.)

THE SCENE

FATHER: *(coming forward with an insinuating manner)* Good afternoon, my dear.

STEPDAUGHTER: *(her head down, frightened)* Good afternoon.

FATHER: *(trying to see her face and noting she is young; a little guarded for fear of being in a compromising situation)* Aha . . . Now, tell me, is this your first time? I mean, the first time you've come here?

STEPDAUGHTER: No.

FATHER: You've been here before? *(the Stepdaughter nods)* More than once? *(she doesn't reply; then with a smile)* Well, then, I don't think it should be too . . . Do you mind if I take off your shawl?

STEPDAUGHTER: *(quickly, with a shudder of disgust)* No, please! Don't!

(She takes off her shawl. The Mother watches the scene intently with the Son, and the younger children who hold on to her; they make a group on one side of the stage opposite the actors. She carefully follows the dialogue and actions of the Father and Stepdaughter, registering a variety of emotions—sadness, dismay, anxiety, shame, horror. At times she turns away and cries.)

MOTHER: Oh, God! God!

FATHER: *(stops, dismayed by the Mother's sobbing, then goes on in the same tone of voice)* Give it to me. I'll hang it up for you. *(he takes the shawl)* But a pretty creature like you should have something much smarter. Would you like me to choose something from the rack here?

KAREN: *(interrupting)* Please, that's my new shawl.

JEREMY: *(angry)* It's all right. He's just acting. Sorry, sir. *(to the Stepdaughter)* Take it back to where you were interrupted.

STEPDAUGHTER: *(to Father)* No, thanks.

FATHER: Don't say no to me. Do it to please me. This is a nice one, isn't it? Paz wants you to take it. He put it there for you.

STEPDAUGHTER: I don't think I could ever wear it.

FATHER: You're worried about what they'll say at home if you come back with a new shawl, aren't you?

STEPDAUGHTER: That's not the reason. *(impatient, petulant)* Can't you see I'm wearing black?

FATHER: Oh, you're in mourning. I'm really sorry. I didn't notice. Please forgive me.

STEPDAUGHTER: *(trying to overcome her revulsion)* Stop. Don't go on. That's enough. Don't blame yourself; I really ought to be grateful to you. Don't think about it any more. And I won't either. *(forcing herself to smile)* In a few minutes clothes will be very unimportant.

JEREMY: *(interrupting, and turning to Scott)* Okay, that's good. Hold it right there. *(to Father and Stepdaughter)* You're doing that very well. That's awfully good. *(to Father)* And then we'll do that scene we talked about in the green room. *(to actors)* I think the scene with the shawl really works, doesn't it?

STEPDAUGHTER: But the best part is still to come. Can't we get on with it?

JEREMY: Be patient—in a minute. *(turning to actors)* I suppose it could use something to lighten it up a little.

SCOTT: Could use a joke.

WILL: I think it needs more tempo.

JEREMY: A little joke and tempo.

KAREN: I don't see anything very difficult. *(to Will)* Shall we try it?

JEREMY: *(to Karen)* Could you do that, sweetie? *(Karen: "Yeah, sure.")* That would be great. *(she goes in the opposite direction)* All right, you're here on the bench with your knees pointing that way and your eyes pointing down.

STEPDAUGHTER: *(amused)* She's not wearing mourning.

KAREN: Oh, but I will be.

CHUCK: And she looks pretty great in the morning.

KAREN: In your dreams, Chuck.

JEREMY: Will you stay out of this, please? Go over there and watch. You might learn something about acting. I doubt it, but you might. *(claps his hands)* All right, let's go. Take it from Will's entrance.

(He climbs offstage so he can see better. The door opens and Will enters with the knowing air of an aging lecher. The playing of the subsequent scene by the actors must

*be very different from the preceding scene, but without
the air of parody. The Stepdaughter and the Father react
in different ways, by gestures, smiles, or protests, to how
different their words sound in the mouths of others.
Tommy acts as prompter, telling the actors what to say
next.)*

SCOTT: Stand by onstage . . . and GO.

WILL: Good afternoon, my dear.

FATHER: *(unable to restrain himself)* My God, no! *(the
Stepdaughter bursts into laughter over Will's entrance)*

JEREMY: *(furious)* Will you shut up? At this rate we'll
never get the bloody thing done.

STEPDAUGHTER: *(coming forward)* I'm really sorry. I
just can't help it. That woman is doing just what
you told her. But if someone ever said "Good afternoon" to me like that, I'd burst out laughing—
so I did.

FATHER: She's absolutely right. His voice, his manner . . .

JEREMY: To hell with his voice and manner. Just shut
up and let us rehearse!

WILL: *(coming downstage)* All I'm trying to do is play
an old man in a cathouse.

JEREMY: And you're doing a very good old man. Go
ahead.

CHUCK: Don't worry, Will, you're a natural.

SCOTT: Go on, same place, Will. Stand by . . . and
GO.

WILL: Good afternoon, my dear.

KAREN: Good afternoon.

WILL: *(imitating the earlier gestures of the Father, trying to see her downturned face, but showing two different emotions—complacency and nervousness)* Aha . . . now tell me, I hope this isn't your first time.

FATHER: *(correcting him instinctively)* No "I hope." Just "Is this your first time?"

JEREMY: Yes, it's a question.

WILL: *(glaring at Jeremy)* I definitely heard him say, "I hope." I wrote it down.

JEREMY: What's the difference? Say "I hope" if you want to. Just keep going.

WILL: Big deal.

TOMMY: Is "I hope" in?

JEREMY: I don't care.

TOMMY: I'll bracket it.

JEREMY: *(Will starts the scene again; Jeremy interrupts)* Will, that's good, but it needs some goosing up. It needs to be more urbane, a little more double-breasted. I'll show you. Watch me! *(he climbs onstage to do the entrance)* Good afternoon, my dear.

WILL: *(to Tommy)* Now he's giving me line readings.

KAREN: Good afternoon.

JEREMY: Aha *(he sniffs)* . . . Now tell me . . . *(he looks at Will to make sure he has noticed how he has looked at Karen's downturned face)* You see what I mean? More debonair . . . a little more elegant.

WILL: Like this? Aha! *(loud snort)*

JEREMY: No, no, the snort is optional. *(once again to Karen)* Now tell me, is this your first time? I mean, the first time you've come here? *(looks again at*

Will) See what I mean? A little more cosmopolitan, more urbane, more Ivy League, a bit more patronizing . . . a bit more . . . Bill Weld, a little less Newt Gingrich. *(he climbs down off the stage)*

SCOTT: Okay, Will. From "Now tell me." Stand by . . . and GO.

WILL: *(continuing)* Aha . . . Now tell me, I hope this isn't your first time.

KAREN: No.

WILL: You've been here before? More than once?

TOMMY: Uh, Will?

WILL: *(screaming with frustration)* What? What? *What!*

TOMMY: Are you finished? It's a two-part question. If you're going by the numbers, you have to wait for her answer. You say, "You've been here before?" She nods. And then you say, "More than once?" It's a two-parter.

JEREMY: Yeah, a two-parter.

CHUCK: One and two.

JEREMY: Okay, Will?

WILL: *(haughtily)* I'm not in the mood now.

JEREMY: Would you rather rehearse *The King Stag*? *(Will sits down immediately)* There you go.

WILL: Now tell me, I hope this isn't your first time?

KAREN: No.

WILL: You've been here before?

TOMMY: Nod.

WILL: More than once?

63

STEPDAUGHTER: *(involuntarily)* Christ! *(she immediately claps her hand over her mouth to stifle her laughter)*

CHUCK: What the hell now!

STEPDAUGHTER: Not a thing. Not a thing.

JEREMY: *(to Will)* Come on, Will, it's your cue.

WILL: Well, then, I don't think it should be too . . . Do you mind if I take off your shawl? *(Will says this line in such a way that the Stepdaughter can't help but break out laughing)*

KAREN: I'm not hanging around here any longer to listen to that woman snickering.

WILL: Me neither! I've had it—up to here!

JEREMY: *(shouting to the Stepdaughter)* I'm asking you for the last time, will you kindly shut the fuck up! I'm sorry. I'm really sorry.

WILL: *(under his breath)* Little bitch!

TOMMY: I think she's really very rude.

FATHER: *(trying to interrupt)* Yes, she has gone too far, but try to forgive her. . . .

JEREMY: Why should we? Her rehearsal manners stink.

FATHER: Yes, I agree, but the scene had such an odd effect on us.

JEREMY: Odd? Why odd?

FATHER: Your actors are wonderful, really fine. I can't tell you how impressed I am by this man *(pointing to Will)* and this woman *(pointing to Karen)*. But don't you see? They're not us!

TOMMY: Of course not. They're actors.

FATHER: They're actors. And they are acting our parts very well, both of them. But that's the problem. No matter how well they act, they can't impersonate us.

JEREMY: But why not? What *is* the problem?

FATHER: It has to do with their being themselves, and not me or her.

CHUCK: This isn't the Actors Studio. We *transform*. And Jeremy's already told you, you can't act these parts yourselves.

FATHER: I agree. I agree.

JEREMY: Right then. So let's stop arguing. *(to the actors)* We'll rehearse this later—by ourselves. It's always difficult when there are authors around. You can never please them.

TOMMY: I'm beginning to think this wasn't such a great idea.

KAREN: Where's Andy Hardy now?

JEREMY: It's a very good idea. Let's continue if possible. This time without the horselaughs.

STEPDAUGHTER: No more laughing, I promise. My best bit comes now, just wait and see.

JEREMY: Okay, then this is where you say, "Don't think about it any more. And I won't either," then you *(to Father)* come in right away with "I understand, yes, I understand." Then you ask her . . .

STEPDAUGHTER: *(interrupting)* He asks? What does he ask?

JEREMY: Why you're wearing black.

STEPDAUGHTER: No! No! That's all wrong. Do you know what he actually said when I told him to ignore what I was wearing? *(Jeremy: "No")* He said, "Well, let's take off your little black dress and get down to business."

JEREMY: Terrific! Wonderful! That'll go down great with our Sunday matinee audiences.

STEPDAUGHTER: But it's the truth.

JEREMY: It may be your truth, sweetheart, but we're after the theatre's truth. Save your truth for Truth or bloody Consequences.

STEPDAUGHTER: What do you have in mind, then?

JEREMY: Never you mind, just wait and see. Just leave it to me.

STEPDAUGHTER: I certainly will not. I know what you have in mind. You want to turn our scene into a saccharine little soap opera. You want him to ask me why I'm in mourning and have me reply with tears streaming down my face that my father died just two months ago. I simply won't have it. The only thing he's going to say is, *(Father speaks: "Well, let's take off your little black dress and get down to business")* And I, still grieving for my father, will go behind that screen there and unfasten my bra with trembling fingers.

TOMMY: How far is she going to go? Hey, wait a minute. There are kids here. Jeremy, we can't have live sex acts onstage, it's against the law.

STEPDAUGHTER: It's the truth. You're hearing the truth!

JEREMY: All right, it may be the truth. And I'm sorry for all you've gone through. But Tommy's right—

66

we simply cannot have Bubbles LeRoux Going
Down on the Titanic. We don't do porno.

STEPDAUGHTER: You don't?

JEREMY: No, we don't.

STEPDAUGHTER: Well then, thank you very much, I'm
off.

JEREMY: Where are you going?

STEPDAUGHTER: I'm off. The two of you have
planned that whole scene out, haven't you? Now I
understand everything. He's only interested in
the part where he talks about his spiritual suffering—but what I want is *my* drama! *Mine*!

JEREMY: *(shaking with anger)* So now it's all coming
out. All you're interested in is your own selfish little story, isn't that right? But it's someone else's
story too. It's his story *(pointing to the Father)*, and
it's your mother's. We simply can't have a narcis-
sistic little bloody star taking over the whole God
damned shooting match. You cannot dominate
the entire play. This is going to be a company
show or nothing. *(the company cheers) (placating her)*
I'm sorry, but I really don't know why you're making such a fuss. Didn't you admit he wasn't the
first man you had at Emilio Paz's.

STEPDAUGHTER: That's true, I suppose. But in a way
he is every man I ever had.

TOMMY: What's that supposed to mean?

STEPDAUGHTER: He was the original cause of all my
later problems. Before I was even born. Look at
his face and you'll know that's true.

67

TOMMY: Look, he's already told you he's sorry. Doesn't that mean anything? Why don't you give him a chance to act out his guilt.

STEPDAUGHTER: But how is he going to act out his guilt if you don't let him act out his shame. The shame after you ask me to take off the dress I wore in mourning for my father—that the woman in your arms is the same little girl he used to watch coming out of school. A grownup woman now, a woman you can buy. *(Her voice is trembling with emotion. The Mother, hearing this, is overcome with suppressed sobbing, then bursts into uncontrollable tears. Everyone is deeply moved. Pause.)*

STEPDAUGHTER: If you want to hear the rest, as it really happened, then ask my mother to leave.

MOTHER: *(with a loud cry)* No! No! Don't let her do it!

TOMMY: Look, lady, it's only us watching—just us. We've been here from the beginning.

MOTHER: This is agony.

CHUCK: But what's the big deal if everything has happened already?

MOTHER: You don't understand. It's happening now too; it's happening all the time. My suffering is not an act. Can't you understand that? That awful moment happens over and over in my mind. And these two children, why do you think they never speak? It's because they can't speak any more, not now. All they can do is hang on to me, keeping my grief alive—but in themselves they don't exist any more. No more. And she *(indicating the Stepdaughter)* . . . she has gone away, lost to me completely. She's only here now for one reason—to keep my suffering alive forever.

68

FATHER: The eternal moment I told you about. She is here *(indicating the Stepdaughter)* to keep me trapped in that moment, the most shameful moment of my life, and for all time. She can't escape her role and you can't rescue me from it. *(long pause)*

JEREMY: But I'm not saying we can't stage that moment. In fact, I think it should be the climax of the first act. The moment when she *(indicating the Mother)* discovers you . . . with her.

FATHER: That's right. Because that is the critical moment, when all our suffering is climaxed by her scream.

STEPDAUGHTER: It's still ringing in my ears! The scream that drove me mad. Play it any way you like. Even with clothes on. Just let me keep my arm bare—only one arm. Because you see I was standing like this *(moves to the Father and lays her head on his chest)*, my arms around his neck, and I saw a vein, a little vein in my arm, throbbing. And that throbbing vein terrified me, and I closed my eyes—like this—and buried my head in his chest. *(turning to the Mother)* Scream, mummy, scream! *(buries her head in Father's chest, with her shoulders raised so as not to hear the scream; she speaks with a suffering intensity)* Scream the way you screamed then!

MOTHER: *(coming forward to pull them apart)* No! She's my daughter! My daughter! *(tearing her from him)* You pig! You disgusting pig! She's my daughter.

JEREMY: *(jumping up and down with enthusiasm)* Oh boy, this is great! This is terrific! And then we have the blackout?

FATHER: *(running to him with excitement)* Yes, because that's exactly the way it really happened!

JEREMY: Couldn't have a better moment for the first-act curtain. Blackout. *(the lights black out, leaving the stage and the actors in confused darkness)*

JEREMY: *(to the booth)* What idiot blew the lights? I don't mean blackout now, I mean blackout later.

SCOTT: Floyd, restore, please.

JEREMY: Yes. *(the lights go back on)* Anyhow, it's a terrific first-act ending. I really think we've got something here!

CHUCK: Jeremy, can we move along, please? It's getting late. What happens in the second act?

JEREMY: Yes, that's next. But first we have to know where the second act takes place.

STEPDAUGHTER: In a garden—the garden behind his house *(indicating the Father)*.

FATHER: You'll need a small pond in the garden.

STEPDAUGHTER: Yes, and some trees. But it won't be possible to play everything in the garden.

JEREMY: Why not?

STEPDAUGHTER: Well, for one thing, that one *(indicating the Son)* always stays shut up in his room, and all the scenes involving this kid *(indicating the Little Boy)* happen in the house.

JEREMY: We can fake that. This isn't a movie. We can't keep changing the set every five minutes.

WILL: They do at the Huntingdon.

KAREN: Our audiences are perfectly capable of accepting an illusion.

FATHER: Please don't use that word. It's very hurtful.

TOMMY: Isn't that our job? To create illusions? To help the audience suspend their disbelief?

FATHER: Forgive me, but that's just the difference between us. For you, theatre is only a game, to create a perfect illusion of reality. But we have no reality outside this illusion, and that should make you distrust your own sense of reality—because what you touch, what you believe today is going to be illusory tomorrow, just like your reality of yesterday.

CHUCK: That's great. I think what he's trying to tell us is that we're less real than him and his play.

FATHER: There's no doubt about that at all.

CHUCK: I have a few doubts.

FATHER: I thought you knew that from the beginning.

CHUCK: You're more real than we are?

FATHER: Doesn't your reality change between today and tomorrow?

CHUCK: Of course it does. It's always changing. Everybody's is.

FATHER: Not ours. Don't you see the difference? *Ours can't change.* It will always be the same because it is already determined, and for all time. That's what's so awful. We are trapped in an eternal reality. That should make you afraid even to come near us.

CHUCK: All right, but I never heard of a character stepping off the page and making speeches.

FATHER: You never heard of it because an author rarely shows you the difficulties of creation. When a character is born, he leads such an independent life that you can conceive of him in a hundred situations the author hasn't written. But imagine what happens when an author leaves a character unfinished, and refuses to let him live in a completed script. Isn't it natural for us to do what we are doing now, here in front of you? We tried so hard to persuade our author, first me, then her *(to the Stepdaughter)*, then this poor mother.

STEPDAUGHTER: *(coming forward as in a dream)* That's true. I would go and tempt him, when he was sitting quietly in his gloomy study in the dark. . . . I would become one of the shadows swarming around the room. . . . Ah, what scenes I suggested to him. What a life I could have had. I tempted him more than anyone else!

FATHER: You certainly did. It was probably your fault he dropped us. You were such a nag, always so demanding. . . .

STEPDAUGHTER: That's the way he conceived me. *(confidentially, to Jeremy)* It's more likely he dropped us because he was getting fed up with a theatre where the public is only interested in cheap, trite, melodramatic little . . .

JEREMY: Insulting the audience now? Can we drop this theorizing and get to the action, please? I suggest we compress the events so the action can flow. It's not possible to show your little brother coming home from school, then wandering around the house, then hiding behind doors, then brooding over his plan. . . . What was the expression you used to describe his plan?

72

STEPDAUGHTER: A plan that would wither him up completely.

JEREMY: I like that. That's a good phrase. And what else did you say? You "see it in his eyes, always burning stronger"—isn't that how you put it?

STEPDAUGHTER: Yes, that's it. Just look at him. *(pointing to him as he stands next to the Mother)*

JEREMY: Yes, that's good. But you also want the little girl playing in the garden, totally innocent. You see that's just not possible.

STEPDAUGHTER: Yes, playing so happily in the sun. It's the only thing left to me, her happiness, her joy over playing in the garden, far from the filthy misery of that squalid apartment where all four of us had to sleep—and she had to sleep with me. Think about that! My contaminated body next to hers—her little arms wrapped around my neck in such love and innocence. In the garden she was so happy, so peaceful. *(Tortured by the memory, she breaks out in a desperate cry, dropping her head on her arms. Everybody is very affected by her. Jeremy becomes very fatherly and speaks to her soothingly, patting her head, and then the Little Girl's.)*

JEREMY: Don't worry, we'll do the scene in the garden. We'll do all the scenes in the garden—and you'll love them all. Juga, juga, juga. *(patting the Little Girl on the head)* Scott, can you get rid of this crap?

SCOTT: Anthony, could you take out the mirror, please?

JEREMY: And give us something for the sky?

ANTHONY: *(exhausted)* For the what?

73

JEREMY: For the sky.

SCOTT: Whatever you've got up there, just bring something in. *(a white drop comes down)*

JEREMY: Not that drop again, for Christ's sake. I want sky. Oh, never mind. Leave it alone; we'll work on it later. *(calling out)* And Floyd, could you give me something on that for moonlight—whatever you've got up there that's blue—something that'll do moonlight. I don't care what it is. *(a wafer moon descends)* Oh, that's perfect! *(a mysterious blue light suffuses the scene as if the actors are speaking in a garden during a moonlit evening) (to the Stepdaughter)* You see, instead of hiding in the house, the little boy can come out into the garden and hide behind the trees. Oh oh, Scott, we need something for trees.

SCOTT: We've got some light booms in the wings.

JEREMY: Light booms are great. And what are we going to do about this pond?

SCOTT: All I can think of is we've got a little blue piece of plastic in one of the roadboxes.

JEREMY: Great. Thanks a lot. *(to the Little Boy)* Come over here, son. Sonny, over here. I'm not going to eat you. *(to Tommy, when the Little Boy doesn't move)* Tommy, you're good with kids, could you deal with this, please?

TOMMY: Sure, where do you want him?

JEREMY: Over there.

TOMMY: Okay, kid, it's time to get up, play a little game now, all right? Move around, you know? Okay, you can follow me over here now. *(the Boy doesn't move)* Come on, it's not really scary, we're just going to play a little game, all right? *(the Boy doesn't move)* What's the matter with this kid, doesn't he ever talk? Well, he's a big boy, he's gotta speak some time. It's getting late, so I'm going to have to move things along a bit, all right? Lady, I'm just going to take him over there. No, really, it's no big deal really. He's just going to be right over here. You'll be able to see him the whole time, all right? *(Tommy tries to coax him into the center of the stage and hold his head up, but his head keeps falling down on his chest)* Come on, don't be a little wimp. *(he coaxes him toward the trees)* Now, you see this pole? You're gonna go right here by this pole. Thatta boy. You see, this is a light pole. When we do plays, we put big lights on this so we can light up the play. But what I want you to do now is pretend it's a tree. You gotta pretend it's a tree. You gotta pretend it's a big tall tree, right? It's nighttime, it's kind of spooky, and you're hiding behind this tree and you're watching all these people do all these crazy things. Okay? You can see them, but they can't see you, okay? You're hiding behind this tree here. That's it. *(Tommy moves back to the actors, shaking his head, as the Boy does what he is told. The actors watch, impressed but a little disturbed.) (to the actors)* Weird kid.

JEREMY: *(to the Stepdaughter)* Look, perhaps we could have the little girl run across, surprised to see him? Maybe that would make him talk.

STEPDAUGHTER: It's no use. He won't speak as long as that character's there. *(pointing to the Son)* Get rid of him first.

SON: *(moving offstage)* My pleasure. I'll get out of here right now. Nothing would please me more.

JEREMY: *(stopping him)* Hey, where are you going? Chuck, Tommy, grab him. *(the Mother, frightened that he is actually going, gets up as if to hold him back, but without moving from her spot)*

TOMMY: I'm sorry, but we have to finish this now.

SON: *(as Tommy and Chuck stand in his way)* There's no reason for me to stay here. Let me go, please, let me go!

WILL: What does he mean, there's no reason for him to be here?

STEPDAUGHTER: *(calmly, ironically)* Don't worry about it. He can't leave.

FATHER: You have to play that terrifying scene in the garden with your mother.

SON: *(quickly, with anger and determination)* I refuse to *play* anything. I've told you that all along. *(to Chuck)* Just let me go, will you?

STEPDAUGHTER: *(to Chuck)* It's all right. You can let him go. *(to the Son)* Well, go ahead. Take off. *(The Son, as if pulled by a strong invisible force, is unable to leave the stage; then he moves to the other side of the stage but again cannot leave. The Stepdaughter, scornfully watching him, bursts out laughing.)*

STEPDAUGHTER: He can't, don't you see? He's stuck here—chained to us forever. I'm the one who leaves—because I can't stand the sight of his hateful face any more. But he's stuck here with his delightful father and a mother who thinks he's the only son she's got left. *(to Mother)* Come on, mummy, come on. You see, she's going to try to stop him. Her need for him is so strong that— look, she's going to try to play that scene with him again! *(the Mother has come close to the Son as*

76

the Stepdaughter speaks her last line; she gestures to show she will play the scene)

SON: *(quickly)* But I won't. I refuse. If I can't leave, then I guess I'm stuck here. But I will not take part in this charade.

FATHER: *(to Jeremy, excitedly)* You'll have to force him.

SON: Nobody can force me to do anything.

STEPDAUGHTER: Stop! Hold on a minute! First, this little girl has to go near the pond. *(she goes to the Little Girl, drops to her knees, and holds her face between her hands)* My sweet little honey, there's such confusion in your beautiful little eyes. You don't know where you are, do you? Well, you're on a stage, my sweetheart—this is a place where people pretend to be serious. They put on plays here—and now we're going to put on a play. Yes, even you. . . . *(she hugs her tightly and rocks her gently for a moment)* But, my darling, my little darling, what a terrible play it is for you! What awful things are going to happen to you! The garden, the trees, the pond . . . *(Scott enters and gently, playfully puts two toy ducks on the plastic)* Oh yes, it's only an imaginary pond. But that's part of the game—it's all pretense here. You might even like a pretend pond better than a real one. But it's only a game for the others—for you, it's terribly real, a real pond, big and beautiful and green, with shadows cast by the trees, where you can look at your own reflection, where there are lots of little ducklings swimming around, shattering your image. Do you want to pet one? *(with a scream that electrifies everybody)* No, Rosie, no. Your mummy isn't watching—she's over there with that selfish creep! And you. *(turning to the Little Boy)* Why are you hanging around here with that pitiful face? It will be your fault if that little girl drowns, you know. *(shaking his arm to make him take his hand out of his pocket)* And what have you got in there? What are you hiding? Take your hand out of your pocket, take it out! *(She pulls his hand out and, to everyone's horror, reveals him holding a revolver. She looks at him with momentary satisfaction, then grimly.)* Where the hell did you get that? *(the Boy, frightened, his eyes wide and empty, makes no reply)* You silly ass. Instead of killing yourself, why didn't you put a bullet into one of them—the father or the son? Get out of here! *(She pushes him toward the trees where he stands watching. Then she helps lift the Little Girl into the pond, where she is hidden. Then she kneels and puts her head and arms on the rim of the pond.)*

JEREMY: This is really getting good. And at the very same time . . .

SON: *(scornfully)* What do you mean "at the very same time." There was no same time. There wasn't any scene between her and me. She'll tell you what happened.

(Karen and Tommy have left the actors to study this scene as if to play the parts)

MOTHER: It's true. I had gone to his room.

SON: My room, understand? Not the garden!

JEREMY: Who cares! We have to change things anyway. I've told you that!

SON: What do you want?

TOMMY: Nothing.

KAREN: Just watching.

SON: Getting ready to play our parts, right?

78

JEREMY: Of course. And you ought to be very grateful.

SON: *(ironically)* Oh, I'm very grateful. But haven't you realized yet that you will never act this play? You're only seeing us from the outside. How could we go on living if we had to look into a mirror that not only froze our images but mocked us with expressions that weren't even ours?

FATHER: You're right! He's right!

JEREMY: All right, Karen dear, Tommy old heart, get off the stage. You're making them nervous.

SON: It's hopeless. I'm not prepared to perform.

JEREMY: Oh, shut up already, and let us listen to your mother. *(to Mother)* Okay, you went to his room, you say?

MOTHER: Yes, to his room. I was frantic. I wanted to pour out all the agony I was feeling. But the moment he saw me come in . . .

SON: Absolutely nothing happened. I took off! I wasn't going to get involved. I have never been involved. Understand?

MOTHER: That's true.

TOMMY: Lady, we have to have the scene between you two. It's crucial to the play's . . .

MOTHER: I'll do it. But if I could only talk to him for a minute and tell him.

FATHER: *(violently to the Son)* Do it for your mother. She's your mother.

SON: I will do nothing.

FATHER: *(shaking him by the coat collar)* For Christ's sake, do as you're told. As you're *told*. Can't you hear her? Don't you have any feelings for her at all?

SON: No, I don't! I don't! That's the end of it!

(There is a general uproar. The frightened Mother tries to separate them.)

MOTHER: Stop it, stop it, please!

FATHER: *(hanging on)* Do as you're told! As you're told! As you're *told*!

SON: *(wrestling with him and finally throwing him to the ground)* What the hell's the matter with you? Are you crazy? Do you want to trumpet our disgrace to the whole world? Well, I'm having no part of it. None! And I'm following our author's wishes—he never wanted us on the stage.

CHUCK: Then why on earth did you come into our theatre?

SON: He wanted to, not me.

JEREMY: But you're here now.

SON: It was his fault. He dragged us all here and arranged with you what to put in the play. Not only what had happened—that was bad enough—but what didn't happen too.

TOMMY: What *did* happen. Did you run out of the room without saying anything?

SON: I did. I didn't want to make a scene.

CHUCK: But then . . . what happened then?

SON: Nothing. I went across to the garden . . .

TOMMY: Go on. You went across to the garden.

SON: *(exasperated)* Why are you making me talk about it. It's terrible. *(the Mother is sobbing and looking toward the pond)*

JEREMY: *(quietly, following her glance and turning to the Son with increasing anxiety)* Is it the little girl?

SON: There, in the pond . . . *(the Little Girl is sinking as the plastic descends and fills with water)*

FATHER: *(on the floor, pointing to the Mother)* She was following him!

JEREMY: And then what happened?

SON: I ran over. I wanted to jump in and pull her out. . . . But I saw something out of the corner of my eye—something behind that tree that froze me with horror. The little boy, he was standing by the tree with a crazy look in his eyes—he was looking into the pond where his little sister was floating on the surface . . . drowned.

(The drop has gone transparent, revealing real trees, a real moon, and a real pond—and the Little Boy standing there with his back to the audience. The Stepdaughter remains near the pond behind the Little Girl; she sobs pathetically, her sobs sounding like an echo. Pause.)

SON: I started to move toward him. But at that moment . . . *(Little Boy raises the revolver to his head, shoots, and falls)*

MOTHER: *(runs with the Father and the Son behind the drop in the midst of panic and confusion)* My son! My son! *(her voice emerges from the confusion)* Help me! Help! *(the lights black out; general confusion)*

TOMMY: I don't think this is part of the act.

JEREMY: Turn the fucking lights back on, for Christ's sake.

EVERYBODY: Floyd, get the lights back on.

FLOYD: *(from the booth)* I've lost all power to the board.

(ad libs of panic from the actors, trying to clear a space and be heard above the din as the actors carry the Little Boy by his feet and shoulders from behind the white drop)

TOMMY: Chuck, get that lamp over here.

KAREN: *(very upset)* He's dead. The poor kid's dead. God, how awful!

WILL: What do you mean the kid's dead? It's all fake. An act. He's not dead, believe me.

TOMMY: No, she's right. It really happened. He really shot himself. His head's blown away.

CHUCK: Don't be silly. It's all part of the play. The kid's alive.

TOMMY: No, he's dead. *(The Little Boy has disappeared. Long pause.)*

WILL: It's an act, a fake.

FATHER: *(voice over)* Not a fake. It's real, my friends, absolutely real.

(The stage lights flicker and then return. Floyd says: "Power's back." Will has checked offstage: "The back door's locked." They look at each other uncertainly. Pause.)

SCOTT: Weirdest trick I ever saw.

TOMMY: That was no trick, Scott. There's real blood on my hands.

JEREMY: There's no blood, Tommy.

WILL: Door's locked.

CHUCK: Wait until Bob finds out we didn't rehearse *King Stag*. Boy, is he going to be pissed.

KAREN: That poor kid.

WILL: It was all a fake. A fake.

JEREMY: *(ceasing to care any more)* Fake? Real? Oh, who gives a damn! I feel like I've been through a wringer.

KAREN: Who were those people? Where did they come from?

JEREMY: Where did they go?

SCOTT: Well, we can't resolve it now. It's 9:30, Jeremy. We have to clear the stage. The Equity day is over. We'll rehearse tomorrow.

JEREMY: Okay, what'll we do tomorrow?

SCOTT: Well, we'd better do *King Stag*. We didn't get to it tonight.

JEREMY: Okay, everybody, we'll meet here at 2 tomorrow and finish up *The King Stag*. Scott, can I get some help cleaning this stuff up? Leave the drop, we'll need it for *Stag*, but get rid of the moon, please.

(The actors wander out of the house, ad libbing their departure—"You want to catch a beer?" "I could use a hamburger." "Let's go to the Sheraton and get a real hamburger." "Can I ride with you?—I don't want to walk alone tonight," etc.)

SCOTT: Jeremy, are you all right?

JEREMY: What?

SCOTT: I said, are you all right?

JEREMY: Oh sure, yes, fine.

SCOTT: All right, well, don't stay here too long by yourself. *(Scott exits)*

JEREMY: *(with Scott, he is the last to remain)* All right, kill the lights. Everything! *(all the lights go out, leaving him in pitch darkness)* Not *everything*! You might have left the work lights on. I almost fell off the stage.

(Suddenly, from behind the white drop, the loading doors begin to rise again, as at the beginning, revealing the six Characters standing as before. Their voices mix with snatches of their earlier dialogue. Father: "We're looking for an author." Stepdaughter: "You could be our play." Father: "Any author will do." Mother: "This is agony." Son: "Leave me out of it." Stepdaughter: "Take me home with you." Father: "We want to live—through you." Mother: "It's happening now. It's happening all the time." Father: "The eternal moment." Son: "I'm an unfinished character." Mother: "My suffering is alive forever." Stepdaughter: "Take me home with you." Suddenly the six Characters fall forward with a loud crash on the floor. They are life-size color photographs.)

JEREMY: *(panicked)* Jesus Christ. *(He runs out of the theatre. Work lights and house lights bump on quickly. Anthony wanders on with a broom, cleaning the stage. No curtain call. The voices follow the audience into the lobby and out the door.)*